The Name Jar

Through the school bus window, Unhei looked out at the strange buildings and houses on the way to her new school. It was her first day, and she was both nervous and excited.

She fingered the little block of wood in her pocket and remembered leaving her grandmother at the airport in Korea. Her grandmother had wiped away Unhei's tears and handed her an ink pad and a small red satin pouch.

"Your name is inside," she had said.

My name? Unhei had wondered.

Again she took out the red pouch to look at the wooden block with her name carved in it. As she ran her fingers along the grooves and ridges of the Korean characters, she pictured her grandmother's smile.

"Is that thing for show and tell?" a boy asked Unhei, surprising her.

Unhei looked up as more kids leaned over.

"No…it's mine," Unhei answered, quickly putting the pouch back in her pocket.

"Are you new here? What's your name?" a girl asked.

"Unhei," said Unhei.

"Ooh-ney?" the girl asked, scrunching up her face.

"Oooh, oooh, oooh-ney!" some kids chanted.

"No, no," Unhei corrected. "It's spelled U-N-H-E-I. It's pronounced Yoon-hye."

"Oh, it's Yoo-hey," the boy said. "Like 'You, hey!' What about 'Hey, you!'"

Just then, the bus pulled up to the school and the doors opened. Unhei hurried to get off.

"You-hey, bye-bye!" the kids yelled as she left. Unhei felt herself blush.

Unhei stood in the doorway of her new and noisy classroom. She was relieved that the kids on the bus had gone to other rooms, but her face still felt red.

"Aren't you going in?" asked a curly-haired boy with lots of dots on his face. "You're the new girl, right?" he asked cheerfully.

Unhei nodded, and before she could walk away, the boy took her hand and pulled her through the door.

"Here's the new girl!" he announced so loudly that the teacher, Mr. Cocotos, almost dropped his glasses.

Mr. Cocotos thanked him and greeted Unhei. "Please welcome our newest student," he said to the class. "She and her family just arrived from Korea last week."

Unhei smiled broadly and tried not to show her nervousness.

"What's your name?" someone shouted.

Her mother picked up cabbage to make *kimchi*—Korean-style spicy pickled cabbage—and other vegetables and meat. She also found some seaweed, Unhei's favorite, for soup. It made Unhei smile.

"Just because we've moved to America," her mother said, "doesn't mean we stop eating Korean food."

At the checkout counter, a friendly man smiled at Unhei. "Helping your mother with the shopping?" he asked.

Unhei nodded.

"I'm Mr. Kim," he said. "And what is your name?"

"Unhei," she answered.

"Ahh, what a beautiful name," he said. "Doesn't it mean *grace*?"

Unhei nodded again. "My mother and grandmother went to a name master for it," she told him.

"A graceful name for a graceful girl," Mr. Kim said as he put their groceries into bags. "Welcome to the neighborhood, Unhei."

That evening, Unhei stood in front of the bathroom mirror.

"Hi! My name is Amanda," she said cheerfully. Then she wrinkled her nose.

"Hi! My name is Laura. Hmm. Maybe not…" Her smile turned down. Nothing sounded right. Nothing felt right.

I don't think American kids will like me, she worried as she began to brush her teeth.

"Ha-ee, ma nem id Shoozhy," she said to the mirror with her mouth full of toothpaste.

The next morning, when Unhei arrived at school, she found a glass jar on her desk with some pieces of paper in it. Unhei took one out and read it aloud. "Daisy."

"That's my baby sister's nickname, but she said you can use it if you want," said Cindy, who sat next to her.

Unhei took out the rest of the paper.

"Tamela," she read.

"I got it from a storybook," said Nate. "She was smart and brave."

Unhei nodded and unfolded another piece. "Wensdy?"

"Yeah. You came here on Wednesday," said Ralph.

"Thank you...for your help." A smile spread over Unhei's face.

Ralph quickly said, "We'll put more names in. You can pick whatever you like—or pick them all, and you'll have the longest name in history!"

At three o'clock, the bell rang for the end of the school day. Unhei looked out the window and saw it was sprinkling. *It's the same rain*, she thought, *but in a different place.* She watched other kids leaving in groups.

"Hey!" a familiar voice called out to her.

Unhei turned around to see the curly-haired boy again.

"I'm Joey," he said. "And you? Don't you have *any* name?"

Unhei thought for a moment. "Well...I can *show* you," she said, and took out the small red pouch. She pressed the wooden block on the ink pad and then stamped it on a piece of paper.

"This is my name stamp," she said. "My grandma gave it to me. In Korea, I can use it as a signature when I open a bank account or write a letter. And whenever I miss my grandma, I use it to fill a piece of paper. Want to try it?" She offered the stamp to Joey, and he carefully inked the stamp and pressed it hard on the paper. The red characters gleamed against the whiteness.

"Wow. That's beautiful," Joey said. "Can I keep the paper?"

"Sure," Unhei said. And then the two of them shared her umbrella as they walked to the school bus.

Every day, the jar got fuller with more names, and Unhei read them all. She found a few names she liked—Miranda. Stella. Avery. They sounded interesting.

"I hope you choose the name I put in," Marco told her at snack time.

"I've put in three more," said Ralph. "Madison, Park, and Lex. They're my favorite street names."

"Maybe you should close your eyes and draw a name," Rosie suggested.

Ralph frowned. "That's silly. What if she doesn't like the name she draws?"

"Well, we didn't get to choose *our* names when we were born, did we?" Rosie argued.

Everyone thought about this.

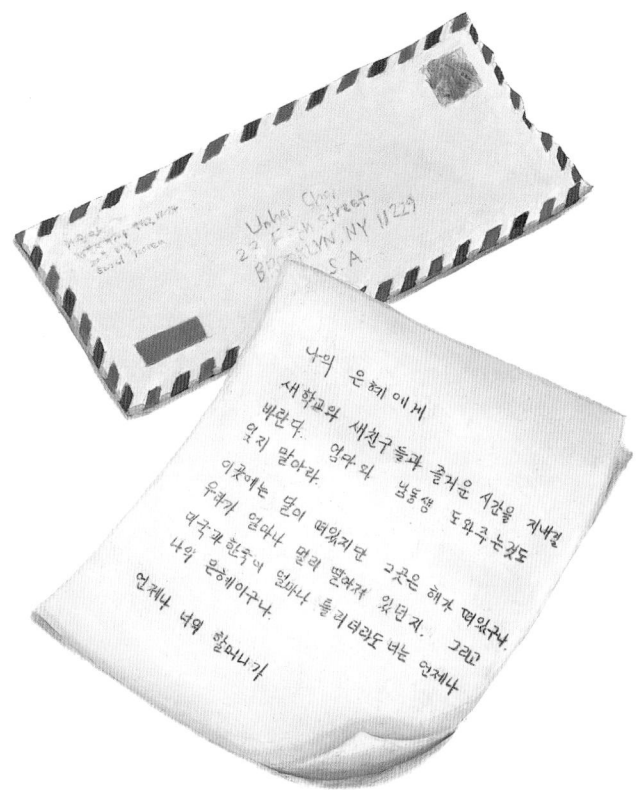

When Unhei got home from school that day, her little brother ran to give her a letter. It was from her grandma.

She opened it quickly. It said,

To my Unhei,

I hope you are enjoying your new school and new friends.

Be sure to help your mother and your little brother.

Here the moon is up, but there the sun is up. No matter how far apart we are and no matter how different America is from Korea, you'll always be my Unhei.

Your grandma forever

Unhei took out her wooden stamp and filled a paper with it. She thought for a long time in front of the bathroom mirror.

On Saturday, Unhei walked to Mr. Kim's store. Mr. Kim was helping a customer, but he looked up and greeted her.

"Hi, Unhei!"

"Hello, Mr. Kim," Unhei replied. She felt as if she was back in her old neighborhood in Korea.

"Hey!" said the customer, turning around. It was Joey.

"Your name is Un-hee?" he asked her with his eyes open wide.

Unhei looked quickly at Mr. Kim, then turned to Joey. She nodded slowly. "Yes. It's pronounced Yoon-hye."

"And it means *grace*," Mr. Kim added.

"Yoon-hye," Joey said slowly and this time perfectly. It made Unhei smile.

"I'll have it ready for you tomorrow," said Mr. Kim to Joey.

"Thank you, Mr. Kim. See you Monday, Unhei," Joey said to her.

He left before she could ask him why he was at the store.

On Monday, Unhei came to class early to look at the names one last time.

But the jar wasn't on her desk. Instead, there was just a single piece of paper. Paper with a name on it. Unhei slipped it in her pocket.

"Where's your name jar?" Ralph asked as soon as he saw it was gone.

"I don't know," Unhei said. It wasn't on Mr. Cocotos's desk or on any other desk. And it wasn't on the counters or any of the shelves.

As other kids arrived, they helped look.

Soon, Mr. Cocotos came in and Ralph shouted at him, "The name jar is gone! The jar with all the names in it!"

"Gone?" Mr. Cocotos replied. With a look of concern, he asked Unhei, "Did you get a chance to read all the names?"

Unhei nodded. She took a breath. "I'm ready to introduce myself," she said.

Unhei wrote her name in both English and Korean on the chalkboard.

"I liked the beautiful names and funny names you thought of for me," she told the class. "But I realized that I liked my name best, so I chose it again. Korean names mean something. Unhei means *grace*."

"Grace! Grace In-hye!" shouted Ralph. Everyone tried to say it. "Yn-ha-e. Unh-yee. Unhae."

Unhei said her name again slowly and clearly. Soon, the kids began to say it better. Even Mr. Cocotos. They applauded Unhei's choice.

"I was named after a flower," Rosie whispered to Unhei.

"Lots of American names have meanings, too," Mr. Cocotos reminded everyone.

When the class was dismissed, Unhei heard her new friends say good-bye.

"Bye, Unhei. See you tomorrow." "G'bye, Unhei."

Unhei said good-bye and then looked around for Joey. But he was already gone.

"Unhei! Unhei! Come downstairs!" Mother called up to Unhei. "Your friend is here!"

Unhei rushed down to see who she meant.

There stood Joey. And in his arms was the name jar.

"Where did you find it?" asked Unhei breathlessly.

Joey looked embarrassed. "Um, well, I took it. But only because I wanted you to keep your own name. And you did!" He reached in and pulled out the names. "Do you want to keep them?" he asked.

"Thank you. I'll keep them as a souvenir," Unhei said happily. Then she pulled out the piece of paper from her pocket. "Do you want this back?"

Joey grinned. "You can keep it. I'll return the name jar to the class. Maybe you could put some Korean nicknames in it for us. Names with good meanings."

"I could do that," agreed Unhei.

"I've already got a Korean nickname," Joey said. "Mr. Kim helped me choose it."

Carefully, he pulled a small silver felt pouch from his pocket. Then he took out a dark wooden stamp with beautiful Korean characters carved sharply into it. He pressed it on the ink pad and then on the piece of paper next to her name.

"Chinku," read Unhei. "That means *friend*!"

And Chinku smiled back.

All rights reserved. Published in the United States by Dragonfly Books,
an imprint of Random House Children's Books, a division of Random House, Inc., New York.
Originally published in hardcover in the United States by Alfred A. Knopf,
an imprint of Random House Children's Books, a division of Random House, Inc., New York, in 2001.

Dragonfly Books with the colophon is a registered trademark of Random House, Inc.

Visit us on the Web! www.randomhouse.com/kids

Educators and librarians, for a variety of teaching tools, visit us at
www.randomhouse.com/teachers

Library of Congress Cataloging-in-Publication Data
Choi, Yangsook.
The name jar / Yangsook Choi.
p. cm.
Summary: After Unhei moves from Korea to the United States, her new classmates
help her decide what her name should be.
ISBN 978-0-375-80613-1 (hardcover) — ISBN 978-0-375-90613-8 (lib. bdg.) —
ISBN 978-0-440-41799-6 (pbk.)
[1. Names, Personal—Fiction. 2. Identity—Fiction. 3. Korean Americans—Fiction.
4. Schools—Fiction.] I. Title.
PZ7.C446263 Nam 2001
[E]—dc21
00039103

MANUFACTURED IN CHINA
39 40

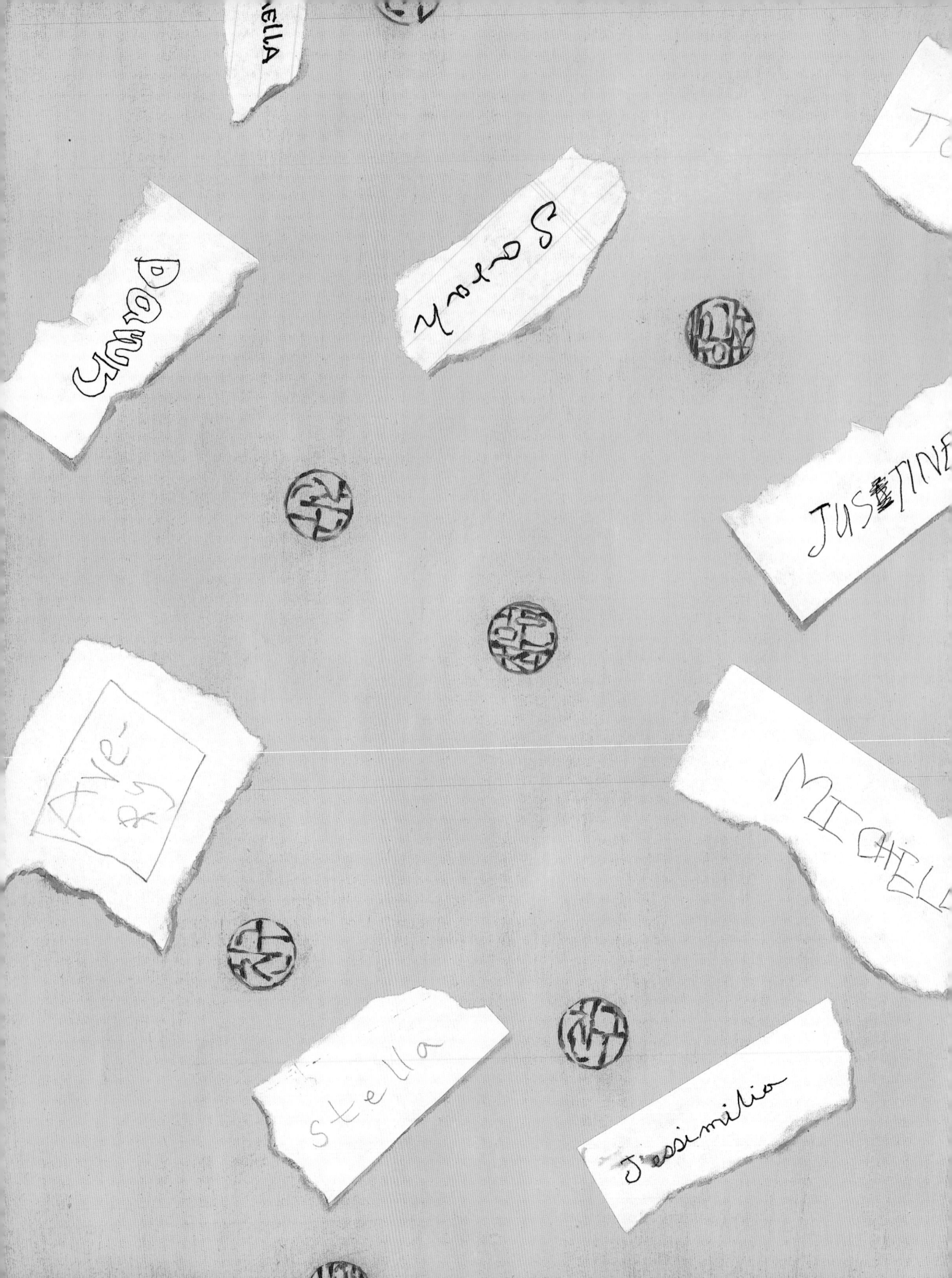

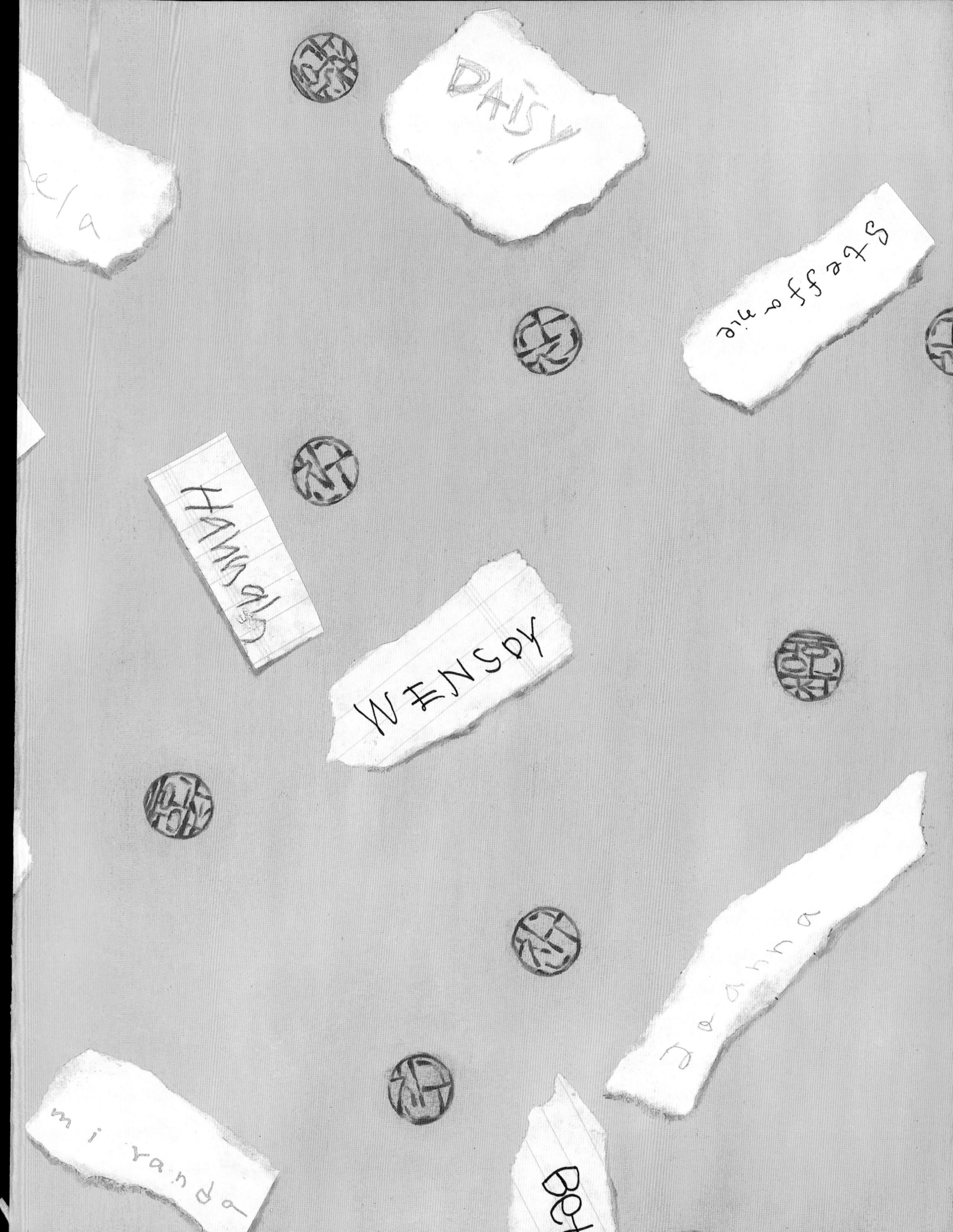

DRAGONFLY BOOKS

Dragonfly Books introduce children
to the pleasures of caring about and sharing books.
With Dragonfly Books, children will discover
talented artists and writers and
the worlds they have created,
ranging from first concept books to
read-together stories to books for
newly independent readers.

One of the best gifts a child can receive
is a book to read and enjoy.
Sharing reading with children today
benefits them now and in the future.

Begin building your child's future . . .
one Dragonfly Book at a time.

For help in selecting books, look for these themes
on the back cover of every Dragonfly Book:

CLASSICS (Including Caldecott Award Winners)
CONCEPTS (Alphabet, Counting, and More)
CULTURAL DIVERSITY
DEATH AND DYING
FAMILY
FASCINATING PEOPLE
FRIENDSHIP
GROWING UP
JUST FOR FUN
MYTHS AND LEGENDS
NATURE AND OUR ENVIRONMENT
OUR HISTORY (Nonfiction and Historical Fiction)
POETRY
SCHOOL
SPORTS

It's a new country, a new town, and a new school for Unhei. So what about a new name?

Having just arrived from Korea with her family, Unhei is anxious about making friends and worried that no one will be able to pronounce her name. Instead of introducing herself on the first day of school, she decides to pick a new name. The only problem is that she doesn't know what name to choose!

A READING RAINBOW BOOK

ONE OF THE CHICAGO PUBLIC LIBRARY'S CHILDREN AND
YOUNG ADULT SERVICES BEST OF THE BEST

"Unhei's reflection and inner strength are noteworthy; cultural details freshen the story, and Choi's gleaming, expressive paintings are always a treasure."
—*The New York Times Book Review*

"Choi draws from her own experience, interweaving several issues into this touching account and delicately addressing the challenges of assimilation."
—*Kirkus Reviews*

DRAGONFLY BOOKS allow children to think . . . to imagine . . . to dream.

The theme of this book is:

CULTURAL DIVERSITY

Need help choosing books your child will enjoy again and again?
Look for other books with this theme:

LOOK INSIDE FOR MORE THEMES!

DRAGONFLY BOOKS New York

www.randomhouse.com/kids MANUFACTURED IN CHINA

US $7.99 / $8.99 CAN

ISBN 978-0-440-41799-6